P9-AQY-463

5-05

THIS BOOK BELONGS TO:

For
Roland
and Fi...

and
Imogen...

and
Giles.

Copyright © 2004 by Lauren Child
First published by Hodder Children's
Books in 2004
First U.S. edition, 2005

All rights reserved. No part of this book
may be reproduced or transmitted in any
form or by any means, electronic or
mechanical, including photocopying,
recording, or by any information storage
and retrieval system, without written
permission from the publisher. For
information address Hyperion Books for
Children, 114 Fifth Avenue, New York,
New York 10011-5690

This book is set in 18-pt Bodoni Classic.

1 3 5 7 9 10 8 6 4 2

Printed in China
Library of Congress Cataloging-in-Publication Data on file.
ISBN 0-7868-5485-5

Visit www.hyperionbooksforchildren.com

HUBERT HORATIO

BARTLE BOBTON-TRENT

LAUREN CHILD

HYPERION BOOKS FOR CHILDREN
NEW YORK

HA CASS COUNTY PUBLIC LIBRARY
400 E. MECHANIC
HARRISONVILLE, MO 64701

0 0022 0241374 2

Mr. and Mrs. Bobton-Trent were frightfully, **frightfully** rich.

They lived in a large luxurious house in London, a swankily swell house in New York, and a marvelously marble house in Milan. They took trips here, trips there, and trips everywhere you could trip to. They bought anything they could think of buying: rare rugs, tiny televisions, crocheted cushions, tailored trousers, plush pajamas, abstract art, china curiosities, posh pets, pungent plants, and strangely shaped swimming pools.

They went out to dinner almost every night, for two, for twelve, for two hundred and two. They dined with the president, the prime minister, and the Queen. They knew simply everyone who was anyone. But, after a while, they began to tire of the same old places and faces, and wanted to meet someone new.

So they decided to have a child.

Mr. and Mrs. Bobton-Trent were
delighted with him. They named him
Hubert Horatio Bartle Bobton-Trent.
Most people called him
Hubert Horatio Bobton-Trent for short,
or **Hubert Horatio** for extra short.

But his parents simply called him *H,* because
they could never quite remember the whole thing.

Remembering things was not one of
Mr. and Mrs. Bobton-Trent's strong points.

ONE day, when Hubert felt he was old enough to tell his parents that he did not like to be called **H**, he telephoned down to the drawing room, where his parents were doing some light entertaining with the Elfington-Learies.

This was when everyone realized that the one-year-old Hubert could not only speak, but could also use a telephone.

WHEN Hubert was two,
Mrs. Bobton-Trent, unable
to find a blanket, tucked
him up under a copy of
The Whispering Weekly,
her favorite gossip magazine.
Upon waking, Hubert
read the magazine twice
front to back and once
back to front.

This was when Hubert found
out he was a pretty good reader.

ONE year later, when the Bobton-Trents were engaged in a furious game of dominoes with their dear friends and next-door-but-one neighbors, the Davenport-Martins, Hubert Horatio fell into the swimming pool.

This was when the three-year-old Hubert discovered he was a natural swimmer.

IN fact, Hubert Horatio Bartle Bobton-Trent
was a natural at almost everything—
with the notable exceptions of
cake baking and flower arranging.

He really had
to work at
those two
skills.

HUBERT
very much enjoyed his
parents' company . . .

. . . and so every night
he would join them for cocoa by making
his way down three flights of stairs . . .

. . . left at the marble bust of Madame Marparcello . . .

His cocoa was
always a little
cold by the time
he got there.

... along the east-wing corridor ... right at the potted palm ... up two flights of stairs, and then three small steps to his parents' bedroom door.

USUALLY he found his parents playing Monopoly in their pajamas.

They took the game very seriously and seldom
played without real money.

All three Bobton-Trents were devoted game
players and committed cocoa drinkers.

OVER the wall, in the next-door mansion, lived
the Saint Bernards—pronounced Ber-*nard*,
emphasis on the *nard*.

Like Mr. and Mrs. Bobton-Trent, the Saint Bernards also had one son who was a child genius.

Stanton Harcourt III was exactly as bright as Hubert Horatio, so, together, the two of them were

He was called Stanton Harcourt III and was Hubert's best friend and a keen table-tennis enthusiast.

probably the brainiest person in whatever country they happened to be in at the time.

HUBERT and Stanton Harcourt III liked
to spend time concocting experiments and discovering
formulas in their homemade laboratory.

Sometimes, just for the fun of it, they would multiply
tricky fractions and then divide them by the square
root of a difficult digit. Other times they would quiz
each other on obscure Japanese vocabulary.

When *they* were *not* doing that they were *playing* table tennis.

ONE Tuesday, Hubert returned from school to find an invitation from his parents. It said:

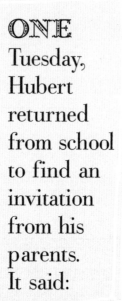

Dearest H,

Are throwing an enormous party and inviting absolutely everyone we have ever met and some we haven't. Please join us in the ballroom.

With love,
Your Parents.

Hubert always enjoyed these parties as he was an exuberant dancer.

However, on this occasion something very odd occurred: halfway through the party, the jelly ran out.

This was highly unusual.

Hubert's parents never ran out of anything.

THE next strange happening
took place when Hubert and Stanton
Harcourt were on the roof, counting
moon craters at dawn. They noticed
Mr. Grimshaw, the butler, handing
the milkman a priceless portrait
of Mr. Bobton-Trent's great-great-
grandfather in exchange for
two pints of milk.

A few evenings later, Mr. and Mrs. Bobton-Trent were entertaining the Butterworth-Trotters and eagerly waiting for Martha the maid to serve them their sautéed scallops. After nearly one hour and twenty-two minutes of no food appearing, Mr. Bobton-Trent said, "Where on earth do you think Martha has got to?"

Hubert
Horatio
quietly
slipped off
his chair
and went to
investigate.

IN the kitchen he found Mr. Grimshaw, the butler, eating cheddar cheese and stale bread.

Mr. Grimshaw explained that, unfortunately, the chef had resigned due to lack of ingredients, Martha and all the other staff had left due to the fact that they hadn't been paid for at least two years, and that he himself would have to resign if he didn't get paid by nine o'clock the next morning.

The immediate problem of what to feed the guests was solved by Hubert, who was a creative chef and quickly rustled up cheese on toast for four.

Delicious.

After serving it to his parents and guests, he went off to his room to see what funds he had in his personal piggy bank. . . .

THERE turned out to be no more than a paper clip and a slightly hairy cough drop. It dawned on Hubert that the Bobton-Trent fortune was in a very bad way.

I.e., there was none.

CLEVERLY,
Hubert managed to sell a slightly broken table-tennis paddle, an ugly bedside lamp, and some back issues of *The Whispering Weekly* over the phone to his friend Elliot Snidge-Combe, thus giving him enough cash to pay Mr. Grimshaw's wages.

THAT night, unable to sleep, Hubert telephoned his best friend and algebra partner for some financial advice.

After some 5.33 minutes of calculations, Stanton Harcourt announced that the only sensible way out of financial ruin was to sell the Bobton-Trent family home. **Hubert Horatio was horrified.**

His parents loved their beautiful mansion. How would they cope if they ever found out they were no longer frightfully, frightfully rich?

What would happen to Grimshaw?

And in any case, where would he put his table-tennis table?

THE following day Hubert and Stanton
came up with an ingenious solution.

They decided to enter

Mr. and Mrs. Bobton-Trent

in various board-game contests.

Hubert's parents were champions of

Chinese checkers,

and could beat anyone on the Scrabble board,

but Boggle was where they really excelled.

They

won

everything.

More often than not, the Bobton-Trents would celebrate . . .

. . . by taking *all* the other contestants out to supper.

IT was Stanton Harcourt who came up with the second brilliant plan. With Mr. Grimshaw's help, the two boys sold tickets, and the Bobton-Trent house was opened to the public.

WOBBLY GEORGIAN SIDE
TABLE, SUPPORTING A
BOBTON-TRENT FAMILY HEIRLOOM
VALUE: PURELY SENTIMENTAL ➡➡

ROCOCO CUCKOO CLOCK
ORIGIN: AUSTRIA
VALUE: NOT SURE, REALLY
⬅⬅

Hubert's parents were astonished when suddenly their afternoon game of

ITALIAN MARBLE BUST
OF MADAME MARPARCELLO
ORIGIN: PISA
VALUE: MAMA MIA! ➡➡

VERY TALL VASE, SLIGHTLY CHIPPED.
(PRICELESS IF UNCHIPPED)

Tiddly Winks was interrupted by a party of sightseers having a good old nose around their home.

SLIGHTLY LEAKY JUG
ORIGIN: SWITZERLAND

GRANDFATHER CLOCK
ORIGIN: HUBERT'S GRANDFATHER.
IN GOOD CONDITION EXCEPT FOR
SOME SQUEAKING SOUNDS
(THE CLOCK, NOT HIS GRANDFATHER)

WOBBLY GEORGIAN
CARD TABLE
HEIGHT: FIVE HANDS

INDIA RUBBER PLANT
ORIGIN: CALCUTTA
VALUE: ABOUT ONE THOUSAND
PENCIL ERASERS

UNFORTUNATELY,
Mr. and Mrs. Bobton-Trent were
delighted by the unexpected guests.
So much so that they invited them
back the following week, and,
of course, this added up to several
hundred people. And just tea alone
for several hundred adds up to . . .
several hundred dollars.

Before Hubert and Stanton
knew it, all the profit from
ticket sales had gone.

It seemed,
after all, there
was only one
solution.

IT was with a heavy heart that Hubert Horatio finally asked Grimshaw to drive him and Stanton Harcourt to the real estate agent.

After several nail-biting seconds, the agent said that he might have a home that the Bobton-Trents could afford. It was excitingly called:

17b Plankton Heights. With great trepidation,
Hubert went home to tell his parents the unfortunate news.

IT WAS
PERFECT.

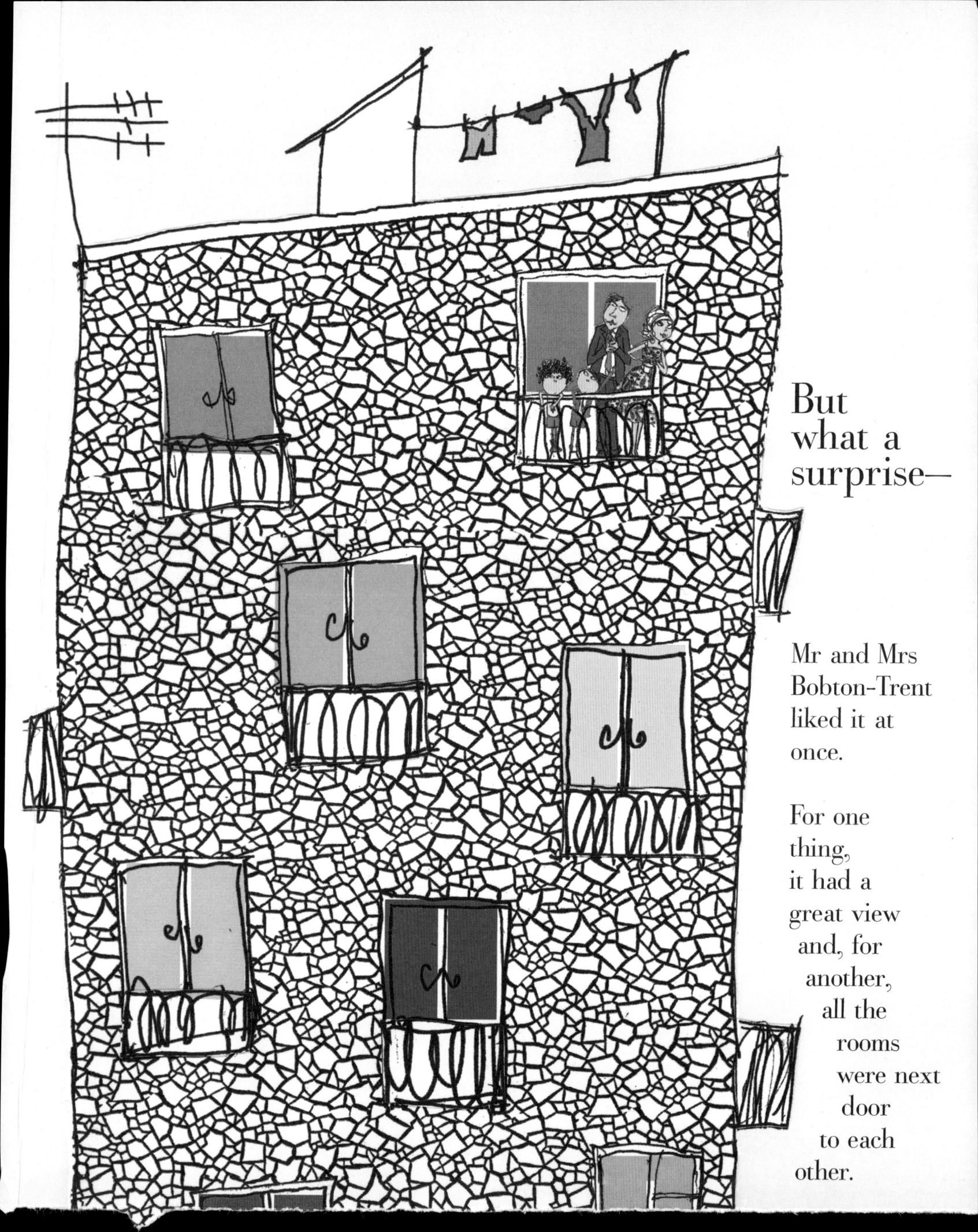

But
what a
surprise—

Mr and Mrs
Bobton-Trent
liked it at
once.

For one
thing,
it had a
great view
and, for
another,
all the
rooms
were next
door
to each
other.

MRS. Bobton-Trent loved that there was always
someone available for a game of Kerplunk.
Mr. Bobton-Trent started his career as doorman,
a job perfectly suited to his social skills. Mr. Grimshaw
retained his job of butler, taking care of all the residents.

And Hubert and Stanton Harcourt III found
the perfect place for the table-tennis table. Hubert's parents
said, "**Hubert Horatio Bartle Bobton-Trent**, you are
a genius for moving us here. We have never been so happy!"

And Hubert realized that being frightfully, frightfully rich was not frightfully important to his parents after all.

AND for the first time ever, Hubert Horatio's
cocoa was still warm by the time he had
walked the short distance to his parents'
room to say *"Good night!"*

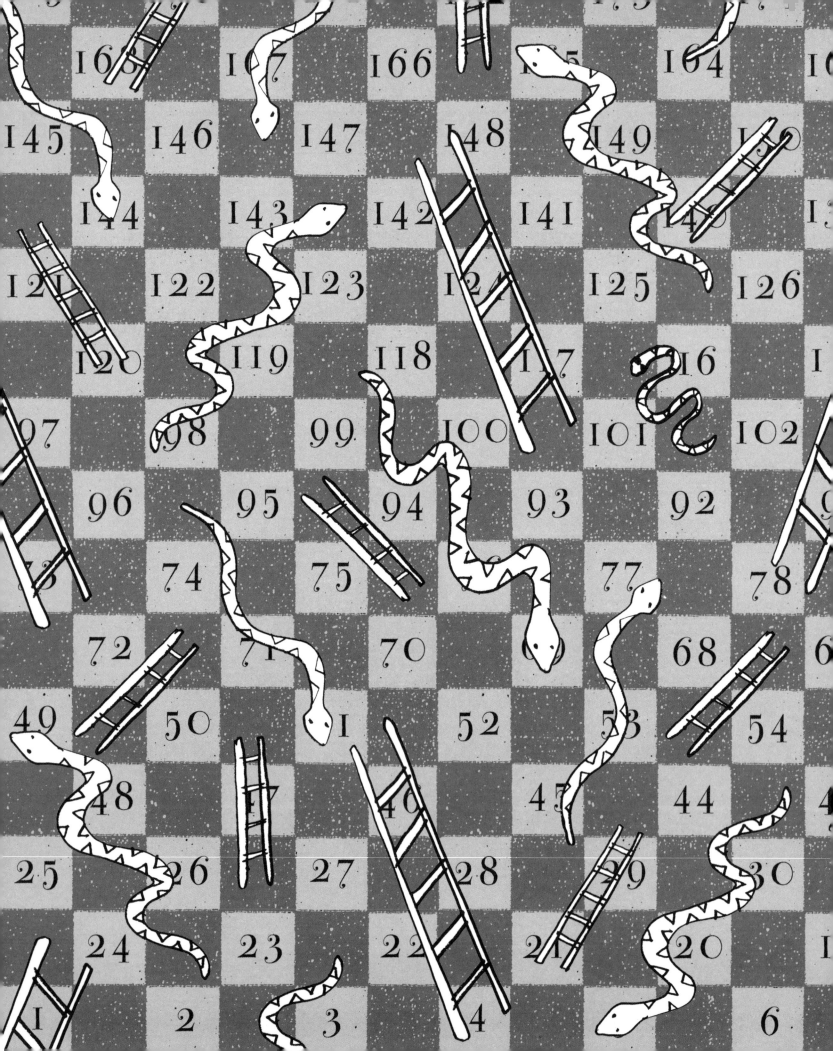